SALLY ANN THUNDER ANN WHIRLWIND CROCKETT

retold by
CARON LEE COHEN
illustrated by
ARIANE DEWEY

GREENWILLOW BOOKS
NEW YORK

Text copyright © 1985 by Caron Lee Cohen
Illustrations copyright © 1985 by Ariane Dewey
All rights reserved. No part of this book may be reproduced or utilized in
any form or by any means, electronic or mechanical, including photocopying,
recording or by any information storage and retrieval system, without
permission in writing from the Publisher, Greenwillow Books, a division of
William Morrow & Company, Inc., 105 Madison Ave., New York, N.Y. 10016.
Printed in the United States of America.   First Edition
1   2   3   4   5   6   7   8   9   10

Library of Congress Cataloging in Publication Data

Cohen, Caron Lee.
Sally Ann Thunder Ann Whirlwind Crockett.
Summary: Sally Ann, wife of Davy Crockett, fears nothing—
and proves it when braggart Mike Fink tries to scare her.
1. Crockett, David, 1786-1836—Juvenile fiction.
2. Fink, Mike, 1770-1823?—Juvenile fiction.
[1. Crockett, David, 1786-1836—Fiction.
2. Fink, Mike, 1770-1823?—Fiction. 3. Tall tales]
I. Dewey, Ariane, ill. II. Title.
PZ7.C65974Sal   1985   [E]   84-7978
ISBN 0-688-04006-3
ISBN 0-688-04007-1 (lib. bdg.)

For Elaine and Bill —C.L.C.

For Harrie —A.D.

Sally Ann Thunder Ann Whirlwind Crockett
lived long ago near the Mississippi River.
Her husband was Davy Crockett.
Now that lady was made of thunder with a
little dash of whirlwind. She wore a beehive
for a bonnet and a bearskin for a dress.
Her toothpick was a bowie knife.

She could stomp a litter of wildcats
and smash a band of starving wolves.
She could outscream an eagle and
outclaw a mountain lion.

She could skin a bear faster
than an alligator swallows a fish.

She walked like an ox and ran like a fox.

She could wade the wide Mississippi
without getting wet.

And she could jump over the Grand Canyon
with both eyes shut.

She could do just about anything.
And nothing on earth scared her.
Nothing!
But she never bragged.
And she never fought a man, woman,
or critter for no good reason.

15

16

Now Mike Fink lived along the Mississippi,
too. He was a bad man, always looking for
a fight. He could beat any man except his
enemy Davy Crockett. Their fights ended in
a draw. And when Mike Fink wasn't fighting,
he was bragging!

One day, Mike walked into a tavern.
He jumped on a table and roared,
"Half of me is wild horse and half
is alligator. And the rest is crooked
nails and red-hot snapping turtles.
I can outrun, outshoot, outfight
any man! If any man says that's not
true, let him step up and fight."

19

No man dared to fight bad man Mike Fink.

But Davy Crockett was in that tavern.

And he was sick of hearing Mike Fink brag.

"You don't scare me," Davy said. "And you

couldn't even scare my sweet little wife,

Sally Ann Thunder Ann Whirlwind Crockett."

Mike roared, "I'll bet you a dozen wildcats

I can **SCARE HER TEETH LOOSE!"**

And the bet was made.

21

So one evening, by the river, Mike found an alligator. He skinned it and crept inside the skin.

Then he crawled along the river. And there was
Sally Ann Thunder Ann Whirlwind Crockett
out for her nightly walk.

Mike crawled toward Sally Ann.
He poked the alligator's head here
and there. He opened its jaws big
and wide. He let out a horrible cry.

He nearly scared himself out of the alligator's
skin. But Sally Ann wasn't scared. Not one
little bit. She just stepped aside as if that
alligator were a dead stump.

So Mike crawled closer and stood up on his hind legs. Then he threw his front paws around Sally Ann.

Sally Ann Thunder Ann Whirlwind Crockett didn't let just any critter hug her. Her rage rose higher than a Mississippi flood.

Her eyes flashed lightning. The night
sky lit up like day. Mike was scareder than a
raccoon looking down a rifle barrel. But he
thought of his bet with Davy Crockett.
He kept circling Sally Ann and wagging his tail.

"That's enough, you worm!" said
Sally Ann Thunder Ann Whirlwind Crockett.
And she pulled out her toothpick.

With one swing, she cut off the head of
that alligator. It flew fifty feet into the
Mississippi River. Then she could see it
was just bad man Mike Fink playing a trick.

"You lowly skunk!" she said. "Trying to
scare a lady out on her nightly walk.
Now stand up and fight like a man."
She threw down her toothpick and rolled
up her sleeves. She battered poor Mike
till he fainted. She was still in a rage, but
she wouldn't touch a man who was down.
So she just walked off.

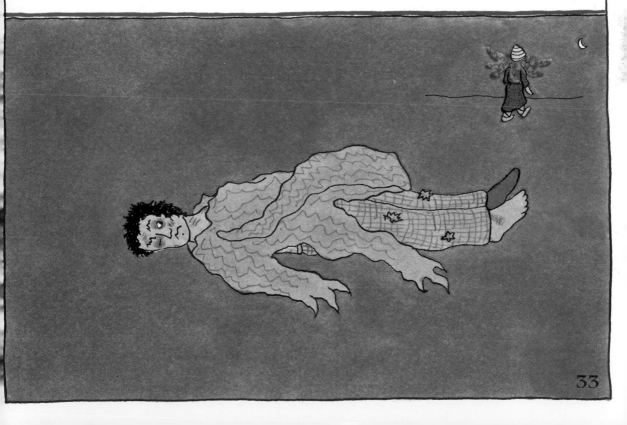

Mike didn't wake up till the next day.
He couldn't tell his friends he had been
beaten by a woman. Instead he bragged!
"I got swallowed by an alligator. But I was
chock full of fight and cut my way out.
And here I am."

Still, a bet was a bet.

So he caught a dozen wildcats

and gave them to Davy Crockett.

But that wasn't the end of it.
One night by the river,
Sally Ann Thunder Ann Whirlwind Crockett
met bad man Mike Fink.

Her rage rose higher than a Mississippi
flood. She lit the sky with lightning
from her eye.

And this time it scared
Mike Fink's teeth loose.

From then on bad man Mike Fink had a mouth full of loose teeth. And every time he bragged, those teeth rattled!